Clifford the BIG RED DOG

Clifford the BIG RED DOG

Story and pictures by NORMAN BRIDWELL

SCHOLASTIC BOOK SERVICES

NEW YORK · TORONTO · LONDON · AUCKLAND · SYDNEY

A hardcover edition of this book is published by Four Winds Press, a division of Scholastic, and is available through your local bookstore or directly from Four Winds Press, 50 West 44th Street, New York, N.Y. 10036.

ISBN: 0-590-08028-8

40 39 38 37 36 35 34 33   0 1 2 3/8
                        Printed in U.S.A.   07

To the real Emily Elizabeth

I'm Emily Elizabeth,
and I have a dog.

My dog is a big red dog.

Other kids I know have dogs, too. Some are big dogs.

And some are red dogs.

But I have the biggest, reddest dog on our street.

This is my dog —— Clifford.

We have fun together. We play games.

I throw a stick, and he brings it back to me.

He makes mistakes sometimes.

We play hide-and-seek. I'm a good hide-and-seek player.

I can find Clifford, no matter where he hides.

We play camping out, and I don't need a tent.

He can do tricks, too. He can sit up and beg.

Oh, I know he's not perfect. He has *some* bad habits.

He runs after cars. He catches some of them.

He runs after cats, too.

We don't go to the zoo any more.

Clifford loves to chew shoes.

He digs up flowers.

It's not easy to keep Clifford. He eats and drinks a lot.

His house was a problem, too.

But he's a very good watch dog.

The bad boys don't come around any more.

One day I gave Clifford a bath.

And I combed his hair, and took him to the dog show.

I'd like to say Clifford won first prize . . . . But he didn't.

I don't care. You can keep all your small dogs.

You can keep all your black, white, brown, and spotted dogs.

I'll keep Clifford . . . . Wouldn't you?